MEN OF HON

Jake

Marteeka Karland, LLC

Marteeka Karland

ISBN: **1546844643**
ISBN-13: **978-1546844648**

CONTENTS

CHAPTER ONE

Jake Carver really missed the days when all he had to do was coddle construction companies and Red Cross personnel in hostile territory. As arrogant and ignorant as those people could be, they could take lessons from Louisville vice. The only reason they were in on this case was because the old man, Jerramiah Hawthorn, had been Navy buddies with the vice captain. What had started as beefed-up security for Jake's brother's comedy club had turned into a full detail. Only they were supposed to do protection only. Without *looking* like they were doing protection only. Which meant they'd been doing investigative work along with protection all while pretending to be background noise.

Which sucked ass.

Everyone suspected their case would eventually end up in Mexico -- and straight to a cartel stronghold. Everyone, that is, but vice. Linda Hawthorn had been the only one of the bunch to see reason, and only because she listened to her father. Again, which was the reason the team from Hawthorn Securities had been taken on board vice for this case. When a retired rear admiral's daughter was in the middle of an investigation that could end in a fate worse than death, one simply didn't say no to a less-than-ideal protection detail. Especially when said retired rear admiral was your boss. Much as Jake hated this kind of work, he did it out of respect.

And he didn't want to lose his job.

And Linda Hawthorn was sex in tight cargo pants that housed all kinds of dangerous objects. Her, he'd happily lose his job for. A hot woman in tight pants with weapons. What's not to love? Add to that, she couldn't be more oblivious to Jake. Well, he *had* been Delta Force. If he wasn't up for a good challenge then he was a pussy.

Speak of the devil.

"I thought I told you to leave the investigative work to the professionals." Linda Hawthorn had an expression of displeasure similar to that of her father. In the general, it put fear into the heart of even the most battle-hardened men. That same look on Linda? Yeah. Instant hard-on.

"And I thought I told you we had to look at this from every angle. Cortez Junior wasn't the leader of this ring. He's the baby brother everyone wishes would go away. We found that out when we got to looking into Scott Dosser's background with him. Can you say 'little fish?'" And there came his second-favorite facial expression. Vexation. More than that, she looked like she could happily throttle him. Discipline play? Only if he turned the tables on that sweet ass of hers.

"My team disagrees," she insisted. "All evidence points to Cortez being the head guy. He's the one getting the paydays. He's the one navigating customs and immigration."

"Which is exactly my point. You think he'd put himself out there so open to scrutiny if he were making the big bucks? Where's his traffic coming from? He can't be here and in Mexico both. And the shipment we recovered that got Dosser in so much trouble definitely came from Mexico. He might *think* he's the head honcho, but I guarantee you there is someone back home pulling his strings."

Her brows knit together, that little line between her eyes becoming more prominent. "So what do you suggest? We just traipse off into Tijuana? Find the Mexican citizen responsible for it and cart his ass back across the border? Cortez is the man we can get. While I concede you might be right in that he's probably got help down south, he's the frontman *here*. He's the only 'fish' Louisville vice is likely to be able to hold on to. I'll take what I can get."

It was hard trying to hold an intelligent conversation with the woman when she fingered the knife strapped to her thigh like a lazy lover. All the blood in his brain went straight to his dick.

"But what if he's not the best we can do?" Jake stepped closer to her as he spoke. Close enough to smell the heady scent of her glossy blue-black hair. God, he wanted to grab a fistful of it and bury his nose there. "What if Hawthorn Securities connections can get close?"

She cocked her head as if unsure she'd heard him correctly. "I'm listening."

"My boss cut his teeth hunting drug lords in Mexico in the eighties and nineties, which

I'm sure you know since he's your dad and all. What you might not be aware of is that he's got a special place in his heart for putting them in small cages and poking them with sticks. As we speak, he's working on a deal with your boss for us to follow the back trail all the way to Mexican border. If he gets what he wants, the city of Louisville will hire us as special detail as extension of vice. We might not be able to cross the Mexican border to get the bastards, but we can trail them through every state in in the union as part of an ongoing investigation."

Linda's lips parted, her breaths growing short. "You're serious about this."

"I am." Jake gave her time to process it all. As expected, her gaze narrowed as the full impact hit her.

"So, why are you telling me this? If our bosses are in agreement, why are we not working this already?"

Jake stood in front of her. He was a tall man, standing over six feet. Linda wasn't a shrimp by any means, but when he wanted to, Jake towered over her. Crossing his arms, he said, "Because you're right that your boss wants the man he's guaranteed to have. Bird in the hand or two in the bush, so to speak. We need you to agree to with us. Convince vice we can do this. If we pull it off, you'll be a hero."

"And if we don't, I'll be the laughingstock of the Louisville Police Department. Forget it."

"Just hold on." Jake chuckled. She'd turned to leave, but he snagged her upper arm to hold her back. "You haven't heard the best part."

"Oh, this I've got to hear." She shrugged out of his grip, crossing her arms and leaning one hip against his desk.

"Our contacts in the ATF got wind of another shipment headed this way. Apparently, Cortez has some competition who wants him out of the way."

"So one cartel giving up another? That's original."

"No. We think it came from *inside* Cortez's organization."

Linda pursed her lips. "Either he's *really* the little brother everyone wishes would disappear, or..."

"They've got a mole."

She looked at him sharply before shaking her head. "No. Not possible. We've tried for months to get inside that group. We never even got close."

"No, but the feds could do it."

"If it were them, why would ATF hand it off to a small-time police force like us? We're not equipped for anything outside the local area."

"They didn't hand it to you. They handed it to us."

"A private security company?" She shook her head. "Even less likely. Why would they think you'd want to be part of this, or even that you'd be able to get the authority to do it?"

Jake grinned. His bombshell. "Because your father thinks the mole is someone he knows. Someone who probably only went to ATF when he or she couldn't contact us, and only under the condition they get us to get to do the extraction."

Linda gasped, her light-coffee-colored skin paling before she sagged against her desk. "Dear lord," she whispered.

"You know, don't you?" All pretense at good humor left Jake. This was what the general had sent him for. "He said you would."

Linda said nothing for the longest time. She just stared at the floor, her breathing ragged. Jake had purposely set her up for this. He needed to know everything -- all of it -- before going in. He trusted the old man, but Hawthorn was first and foremost an admiral. Keeping secrets was second nature to him.

She opened her mouth to speak, then shut it again.

"I'm not doing this until you tell me everything, Linda." No sense letting her think she could bluff her way out with half-truths. "Much as I want this scumbag, I want to come home to my family even more."

"What did the admiral tell you?"

"Nothing. Only that you'd know the significance."

"I need to talk to him."

"Before you talk to me?" Jake chuckled. There was no humor in his voice. "No fucking way. You tell me everything now, or I take my happy ass outa here."

"If he orders you to go, you have to," she said weakly. "You can't disobey a direct order."

"I ain't in the service anymore, sweetheart. I can do any goddamned thing I want. I *work* for your father. It's a job I can quit any fucking time."

Finally, she met his gaze. "What do you know about the rear admiral?"

"I know he's fucking smart."

"He did covert ops in the nineties as part of a special team put together from different branches of the military," she began. "He spent months at a time in Mexico, infiltrating one cartel after another. Always low to mid level. Nothing too outrageous so he could get just enough information to make an arrest, or to leak to a rival cartel. Anything to destabilize the system. To keep things shifting. It was his job. A handful of men kept this going for months. Always changing their appearance, their location... they became completely different men. All they had to rely on was one another and only in extreme circumstances. They couldn't completely extract themselves without risking being compromised. Not until they were pulled out completely.

"Then, after he gained entry into a particularly powerful cartel, he fell in love. Just so happened the woman he fell in love with was the daughter of this cartel's leader, Manuel de la Huerta. Naturally, things didn't end well."

"What's all this go to do with the current situation?"

Linda sighed, turning away from Jake to stand next to the office window. His office at Hawthorn Securities was small, overlooking a side street in a middle-class commercial area of Louisville, Kentucky. Outside, dumpsters lined the brick wall across the alley and litter peppered the street. What she hoped to see as she stared down at the street below, Jake had no idea. Was she remembering something painful? Linda was in her late mid to late twenties. She had been born during the time she spoke of, but it was obvious some knowledge haunted her.

"Look," she said, her gaze still firmly on the street below. "This may have nothing to do with anything. I really think you should get my dad to tell you this. If he won't, then it's really not my story to tell."

"*You'll* tell me," Jake said. He didn't touch her or even move toward her, but he willed her to meet his gaze in the reflection of the window. "The Old Man is adept at keeping his secrets. You, I can read like a book. I want it from you."

Naturally, that miffed her. He could see it in the way her mouth tightened, but she still had a haunted look about her. "You don't know anything about me, Jake Carver."

"I know whoever the mysterious informant is he's linked to you in a very personal way. I know Hawthorn is desperate enough to make an extraction whether or not his informant wants out. And I know you're very uncomfortable. So tell me, sweetheart, what exactly about you and this situation am I misinformed about? Because if I'm risking my life, I'm damned well going to know why."

Finally, Linda turned to him. "The informant is my half sister. De la Huerta found out about my dad. That he was a plant. By that time, Louisa had given birth to my dad's first child. He'd planned on escaping with her and the baby, but de la Huerta got the jump on him. In the ensuing firefight, Louisa was shot by her father's own men. Dad managed to save my sister, but his beloved Louisa was dead.

"Once back in the states, he accepted a promotion and moved his way up in rank within the Navy. He married a Hispanic woman and had the paperwork drawn up to show his new wife listed as his daughter's mother. A year later, I came along. It wasn't until about seven years ago the truth came out within our family."

"I take it your sister wasn't happy?"

"Just the opposite. Our mother was dying of breast cancer. It was one of the last conversations she had with us. She assured Esperanza that she'd always loved her as a daughter, that she couldn't love her more if she'd given birth to her. She knew that because she'd given birth to me and had loved me with all her heart." She hesitated again, but Jake let her work through it. Obviously she was taking great care how to word her next thought. "Esperanza told me a few days later she needed to find out some things about her Mexican family. She knew it wouldn't be easy, and that it would likely be dangerous. But one day, she just... vanished. Even Dad's extensive network of information couldn't find a trace of her. He's been looking for her ever since."

"So, this is the first time he's had contact with her?"

She raised an eyebrow. "*Has* he made contact with her? You said the message came through the ATF."

"I don't believe he has," Jake acknowledged. "This is all assumption. The ATF guy could be lying for all I know."

"Then you might want to find out if the admiral even believes it was Esperanza who contacted him."

"Oh, he believes. Apparently, he's got the whole team in a snit."

"I'm assuming he has a plan?"

"He does."

When Jake failed to elaborate, Linda raised an eyebrow. "Well?"

"Well what?"

She rolled her eyes, giving that little exasperated sigh that drove Jack crazy. If she knew the thoughts he was having...

He'd clear his desk with a swipe of his arm and take her there. Hard and fast. Jake longed to see just how high he could take her before she lost that tight control she held on to. With a grin to himself, Jake bet she'd be like a wildcat in bed if she ever lost herself. He could just imagined her scratching those little nails down his back, digging into his ass...

"Earth to Jake."

"Huh? Oh, yeah. The old man wants us to take a small force. Maybe three of us. ATF gave us a starting point, but I'm sure there will be more to it than one meeting place."

"Is it inside Mexico?"

"Just. A little place called Negales. There is a data-wire factory there that ships goods into the U.S. They think it's partially a front. The company is legit. Unfortunately, they employ several of the Cortez cartel in that factory. We think that's the way Cortez is getting drugs across the border."

"And my sister?"

"If it's her who contacted the ATF, she'll be close by. Your father thinks she wants out."

"You have a different opinion?"

"I am of the opinion that everyone in that place is our enemy until proven otherwise." Jake met her gaze steadily.

"Who did you have in mind to go?"

"You. Me. Gunnar."

"Why you? And Gunnar is way too damned big to blend in. I've at least got the heritage."

"Gunnar because he insists. Me because I'm fluent in five languages, including Spanish. You because she's your sister. Your father's daughter. He wants you there, and you have a right to be there."

She was quiet a moment before speaking again. "Gunnar doesn't want you going alone, and he doesn't trust me, does he?"

Jake hated admitting the truth to her but refused to lie. "No. But Gunnar doesn't trust anyone outside the family."

"Kinje, Noah, and the others aren't family. Kinje is Asian, and Noah has Native American roots. They aren't your brothers."

This was something Jake wanted to drive home to Linda. He intended for her to be part of their family... as his woman. She had to realize why he, Rafe, and Gunnar accepted the others as part of their family. "They are as much my brothers as Rafe and Gunnar. We're a team. A family. We have each other's backs. We watch over one another. Our team has been through hell together. More than most families ever experience. Amanda -- Rafe's woman -- is as much a part of that unit as Rafe is even though she's not part of the team."

"What's that got to do with me?"

"When this is over, you're going to be one of us. I'll see to it."

"You've lost your mind!" Linda clenched her fist, actually thumping the edge of his desk for effect. "I'm vice. Not military. I have no desire to be military!"

"Police work is just a step away. Your specialized training makes you a good addition."

She pointed a finger at him. "I have a job -- a life -- here. All on my own. I don't need or want to be part of your team. In fact, you guys are butting in on my investigation. And you suck as investigators."

Jake shrugged and grinned at her. "Maybe. But you're interested. Tell yourself you're not, but I'm willing to bet you'd love to join up just for the chance to play with explosives and bigger guns."

CHAPTER TWO

The son of a bitch was right. Linda wanted
in on this. Not just the chance to go after her
sister but the whole package. When the
Hawthorn Security team had muscled their way
into their operation at Rafe's club, Linda
experienced firsthand what it was like to be
part of an elite team of warriors. There hadn't
been much fighting until later -- which she
hadn't been a part of -- but just the planning
and execution of an operation with so many
variables had sent a thrill coursing through her.
It was what she'd been trained for yet hadn't
had much of an opportunity to actually do. The
department being what it was, women were
there to meet a quota most times. Jake and the

other men on his team had expertly planned the operation while inviting and even asking for *her* opinion. For the first time in a very long while, Linda had felt like part of the bigger scene.

Everything had gone exactly as planned. They had maneuvered their targets to a hall safely away from innocents in the club. True, her whole team had helped in the planning, but no one had been fooled into thinking they'd had more than a cursory involvement in it. Linda had *loved it*.

"Say I agree to this idiocy. Gunnar doesn't play well with others, and I don't like him in the least. He's obviously the leader of this team. What makes you think he'll even consider letting me in?"

"Because you're going to prove yourself on this mission." Linda opened her mouth to tell him she didn't have to prove herself to anybody, and he raised an eyebrow, giving her that cocky grin that set her heart racing. "And he'll prove himself to you."

This was the *worst* idea. Like ever. Even as Jake stood there grinning at her, Linda knew she was going to agree. Though she'd prefer to go after her sister alone, she wasn't stupid. She didn't speak Spanish, and she'd never even been to Mexico. She'd be at a distinct disadvantage.

"Do you know the area where we're going?"

Jake nodded. "Nogales, Sonora is just across the Arizona border into Mexico. It's not a bad place. Relatively calm. Hell, they even have a Kentucky Fried Chicken."

"I've never been there, but from what I understand there are several U.S. plants there." Linda's heart raced. Was she actually about to find her sister? After all these years?

"Yes. But our factory delivers their goods – data wiring – to Indianapolis, Indiana... by way of Kentucky. Same company has a plant in Monticello, Kentucky that does their quality checks. Each shipment stops at that plant before going to Indianapolis. From there, they go to Louisville where they drop off their contraband, and the drivers have a straight shot to their destination. We think the Cortez cartel is getting their drugs in through the shipments of wire."

Linda hissed out a breath. "That's... far fetched. The cartel using an American company to ship their drugs?"

"Not really. If they had someone fairly high up on the inside in both U.S. plants, it wouldn't take much to pay off a Kentucky local or two to make sure certain containers were left alone and got to where the next guy in the chain could pick them up. Also, consider this. In the past six months, reported heroin overdoses have increased over one hundred percent in cities in Kentucky from Monticello to Somerset, all the way to Louisville and the surrounding areas." Jake pointed at her for emphasis. "There's your highway."

She blinked. The full implication of what he'd said hit her. "How long have you been working on this?"

"Since the ATF first came to the old man a couple of weeks ago. Hawthorn put our team on it and we've been *investigating* the information given to us. With your sister's help we might just be able to shut this avenue down."

There was no way to hide her shock and surprise. "Did I say you guys were poor investigators?"

"I believe you said we sucked." There was that sexy grin again. Linda nearly groaned aloud.

"Smug bastard," she muttered. "So what's the next move?"

"Noah and Tyson followed the trail to Monticello where he confirmed the supply chain in Kentucky starts there. He's scouting ahead to Arizona following the suspected trail to see if it is indeed the route they are using. But he's also going with the intent of fact-checking what the admiral received from your sister. The last thing we want is to walk into a trap."

"You think he can spot a trap that well thought-out?"

The look he gave her said, "Bitch, please." Fortunately for him, he didn't actually voice it like that. "Noah Stein's father comes from the Tohono O'odham Nation in Arizona. Noah spent time as a Shadow Wolf there doing nothing but tracking smugglers from Mexico. If anyone can do it, it would be Noah."

"Seems a little convenient, don't you think? Possibly the one person in this whole state who would be able to follow a trail like this. My sister's message getting to my father -- your boss -- only weeks ago when she'd been away for years. Doesn't this make you just a tiny bit uneasy?"

"It makes me extremely uneasy," Jake answered without hesitation. God, she loved that about him. Jake never pulled any punches and always told the truth even when she knew it would be in his best interest to lie through his teeth. "Makes Gunnar uneasy too. Another reason he's going along."

"Nice. What about Tyson? He have any supernatural powers I need to know about?"

Jake grinned. Fuck! The man could melt panties at a hundred paces with that grin. "Na. He's the muscle. Noah gets into trouble, Tyson gives them hell until they can get out or we get there to help them out."

Other than Gunnar, Tyson was the largest man Linda had ever seen. Where Noah was wiry and lean, Tyson was heavy, bulky, solid muscle.

Then there was Jake. Who was just about perfect. While he was big and all muscle, he wasn't overly bulky. He still towered over her five-foot-six frame. When he looked down at her -- like he was doing now -- he always looked straight into her eyes. She couldn't decide if his eyes were green or blue, but they were mesmerizing. Linda always knew she had his full attention.

"So, I'm assuming we're headed to Arizona. What's the plan once we get there?"

"Noah will fill us in more thoroughly once he makes it there. He said so far, the trail is tenaciously following the interstate. He's still taking time to go off the route to look for signs it's a ruse. As he puts it, intelligent people don't usually leave that big a trail unless it's a diversion."

"When do we leave?"

"Tonight. It's a twenty-six-hour drive to our Arizona crossing point. That will put us there just after nightfall tomorrow. We can get our local update and layout from Noah, then get a little rest before planning our next move."

Traveling all the way to Arizona in a vehicle with Jake. Thank God Gunnar would be there too. Linda didn't trust herself not to make a move on Jake otherwise. He was a thorn in her side, a pain in her ass, and possibly the biggest player she'd ever met, but the man was seriously hot. How could any red-blooded woman keep her hands off him? Which was the whole problem with Jake. She *had* to keep her hands off him.

Just as the thought crossed her mind, Jake moved closer to her. That slow, lazy swagger was nearly her undoing. He wore casual clothing -- jeans and a button-up shirt -- but he wore it like a boss. Thick, strong thighs, lean hips, a broad chest, and bulging arms all beckoned her like a moth to a flame. If she could have picked any man in the world for physical beauty, it would have been Jake. Combined that with his protective tendencies and she was a total goner. Too bad he didn't have the same desires. The man could have -- and often did have -- any woman he wanted.

Linda knew she was a good-looking, even sexy woman. Given they were working together *and* he intended to make that a more permanent situation, *and* she didn't sleep with co-workers, there was absolutely no chance in hell to sample that luscious body.

"Should be an interesting operation," he drawled. That sexy roll of his words send shivers down her spine straight to her cunt. "Might require some undercover work."

"You're a bastard, Jake Carver," she bit out. "You keep to yourself, and I'll do the same."

And there went that panty-melting grin. "What? All in the name of the job. I might have to pretend I'm selling you to them to get us in. Isn't that undercover work?"

With a scowl, Linda pivoted around to exit the office. What else could she do? If she stayed there, she'd do something crazy like slap his handsome face. Or kiss him until *he* surrendered to *her*. Neither seemed like a sound option.

"Whoa there, sunshine," he said, snagging her arm and pulling her back. He maneuvered her close enough to be all up in her personal space. "You're not leaving yet."

"Why the fuck not?" She let her anger show. "This isn't funny. This is my sister. I'm not playing some kind of twisted sex game with you. Not to pass the time on a lengthy trip. Not as a prelude to some kind of perverted sexual relationship. And I have no intention of leaving vice once this is done. I'm perfectly happy where I am."

"Ok. First of all, we've already established you want to play with bigger guns and explosives -- which is sexy as fuck. It's in your makeup. Second, you don't know me, so you have no idea why I'm flirting my ass off with you. Third, and this is really the most important of the three, you *will* be in my bed before this operation is over. We're going to have nasty, dirty, sweaty sex in every position you've ever dreamed of. When it's over, we'll move from the bed to the backyard pool. From there, we'll try parking and see just how good an investment that Excursion I bought was. In each event, sex will be front and center. *But*, I will never -- *never* -- do anything at the expense of getting your sister back and closing down this drug highway. I expect you to put the mission first, too. I also expect you to work as hard as you can to figure out where you're going to fit in with our team, because you belong there. I know it. You know it. Accept it."

The heat in his voice! The heat in his eyes... God, the man was intense! He meant every single word he said -- she could see it plain as day. He fully intended to fuck her senseless, and it might be starting right now. Linda was sure she should be mortified or angry or... something. Instead, she found herself going weak in the knees. Did that whimper come from her? It must have, because the growl definitely came from Jake as he pulled her into his arms and brought his lips down on hers.

Linda raised her hands to push at his chest. Found herself sinking her nails into the heavy muscles there instead. The second Rafe took complete control of her mouth, Linda simply lost her rational mind. All that mattered was kissing him back. Taking what she'd wanted since the first day she'd seen him.

Jake didn't wait for her to surrender to him. He swept in like a conquering Viking or some shit, taking what he wanted from her. Which, apparently, was her sanity because Linda kissed him back with all the lust she possessed. She forgot why this was a bad idea, why she'd never intended to get involved with Jake on a sexual level. The sensations alone were enough to sweep her along for the ride. Add to that his naughty declarations in that sinfully sexy voice, and there was no way she could resist.

Before she fully realized what she was doing, Linda threaded her fingers through his hair to position him where she wanted him. There was a need in her to control this thing between them. Probably to preserve herself. Unfortunately, as much as she *wanted* control, Jake *possessed* control.

He pulled her to him roughly, deepening the kiss even when she nipped his bottom lip with her teeth. The sting only seemed to fuel his lust even more. For her part, Linda knew there was no way she got out of this office without fucking Jake -- until neither of them could stand, if she could help it.

As if he read her mind, Jake growled before swiping a hand over his desk, scattering the contents as he lifted her to set her on the surface. Linda willingly spread her thighs when Jake wedged his hips between them. She urged him closer, tried to deepen the kiss, but Jake fisted her hair and pulled her back. Looking down into her face, Jake looked like a man on the edge of his control. His eyes were wild with the same lust she felt coursing through her body, but he seemed to be determined to rein himself in. His lips were curled in a snarl, but he didn't move away from her. In fact, he pulled her closer, wrapping his free arm around her body tightly.

"Can you feel the pull between us?" His voice was husky, needy. Sexy. "This is why you're going to do exactly what I tell you to do. Use this mission as an opportunity to get to know me, Gunnar, Kinje, and Noah. You *will* find where you belong with us so you will always be with me. I will always have your back and know you're safe."

"Is that the only reason you want me on your team? Because you think I can't take care of myself?" That statement tasted like soot. Not only was Linda a capable woman, she was part of a specialized force in a large police department. She was more than capable of taking care of herself. And, dammit, she wanted Jake to want her as much as she wanted him. Not to use sex as a means of controlling her.

His grip on her hair tightened as he tilted her head back more so she had to look straight into his eyes. "You listen to me, Linda." His blue-green gaze blazed with intensity and fury. If that look wasn't enough to convey his displeasure with her, the growl in his voice was. "This has nothing to do with your abilities. If I found you lacking, there is no way I'd allow Gunnar to offer you a place on this team. I'd still keep you, but you'd be safely tucked away with your little vice squad." His lips pulled away from his teeth to bare them at her, a show of aggression. "Understand me, Hathorn Security is an elite paramilitary force. We don't let inferior soldiers in our midst. You still have things to learn, but you have what it takes. Which means you're intelligent, capable, and definitely not in need of a babysitter." He pulled her closer so they were mashed against each other now. So close Linda felt the hard ridge of his cock pressed against her pussy. Even through their clothes it burned her like a fucking brand. "I have no need to keep an eye on you. But I do have a need to make sure the rest of your team is as capable as you are. As much as I admire the boys in blue, not everyone you work with has the mettle to be there, and it goes against my nature to see you have to depend on an inferior soldier at your back. That's suicide."

This was a side of Jake she'd never seen before. He was usually the fun-loving brother. The one the others depended on to keep them all sane when the situation became too intense. She'd noticed it at Rafe's club when they were gathering intel on Cortez and Dosser. This new facet gave her pause. It also made her stomach flutter and her panties wet.

"I can take care of myself," was all she managed.

"So can everyone on our team. But we're stronger together. We'll be even stronger with you to count on." His response was vehement. Without hesitation.

That was something she hadn't counted on. Could he really want her on the team because of her skills? "You know I don't date co-workers. If we're on the same team at Hawthorn Security, we're not sleeping together."

He gave her a little shake. "One has nothing to do with the other!" His fist pulled at her hair, a warning as he pulled her face closer to his. "We're a team. On and off the battlefield," he snarled. "Understand?"

She didn't. At all. "Are you going to keep blabbing or kiss me?" It was all she could think of at the moment. Anything else was too much for her lust-filled brain to attempt to process.

With a savage growl, Jake descended on her mouth, taking her with a hunger that thrilled Linda to her toes. His tongue swept inside to tangle with hers. Linda tried to war with him for dominance, tugging his hair the same as he did hers, trying to angle him where she wanted him. He was having none of it. With brute force, he dominated her, taking what he wanted even when she finally relaxed and let him have it willingly. What else could she do? His kiss was masterful. Demanding. Jake's inherent nature called to something primitive inside her, taking her to a place she never knew existed.

Linda tried her best to move on Jake, to rub against that thick bulge trapped between her legs. She knew this wasn't the right place or time, but hadn't she known she wasn't letting Jake out of this room without fucking him silly? Wrapping her legs around his waist, she raised herself up with that leverage and put one hand behind her to brace herself on the desk. Jake let her pull away from him as she moved, sliding up and down his rigid length. The friction was incredible, and she let her head fall back, her long, dark hair falling behind her in a wave.

"I love the way you look when you're lust-drunk," Jake rasped out. "So fucking beautiful..."

She wanted to respond -- needed to -- but words wouldn't come. All she could do was keep moving. Her breath came in ragged gasps, the need to come nearly overwhelming. Her entire world narrowed to the man in front of her and his power over her. In that moment she didn't care. Couldn't care. Later. She'd regret it later.

With a brutal yank, Jake pulled her as close to him as she could get. Linda instinctively wrapped her arms around his neck, sobbing into his flesh. The pleasure was so intense all she could do was hang on.

Then he stopped. Hands on her hips, he sank his fingers into her flesh to hold her still. "No," he rasped gruffly in her ear. "Not until I say. And not today."

"You fucker!" she gasped.

"Absolutely."

He held her, still wrapped tightly in his arms. Linda trembled uncontrollably but, no matter how much she wanted, she couldn't make herself continue to grind against him for relief. How did he have such power over her? Why did it thrill her?

They stayed like that for several moments while Linda came down from an adrenaline-laced high. It was like having the ultimate prize just in front of you only to have it disappear just as you reached it. The feeling was not in the least fulfilling, and it took a long time for her body to process the fact that she wasn't coming.

Finally, Jake helped her off the desk, his hands steady on her waist so she didn't do anything seriously stupid. Like fall on her fucking face.

"What are you doing to me?"

He gave her that cocky grin she both loved and hated. "It's my sex appeal. I've heard it's just too much for the mere mortal woman."

She opened her mouth to retort, but he chuckled. Was it her imagination, or did he sound a bit strained?

"Go," he said. "Pack a bag. Light. Catch a nap if you can because we leave tonight, and we don't stop until we get to the Mexican border."

Linda knew she should say something. Anything other than agreeing with him. But there was no forming a coherent thought. All she could do was nod her head before leaving. As she glanced at him from the doorway, Linda had a moment to wonder how the fuck she was going to do this without losing a little bit of herself in the process. If she fucked Jake Carver, there was no going back. He had imprinted on her body and soul. If he took her fully, she'd always belong to him whether he belonged to her or not. Which presented a problem because, in those brief moments they'd taken pleasure in each other, Linda had realized that she did, indeed, want Jake Carver for her own.

CHAPTER THREE

The trip had taken them close to twenty-four hours. It passed quickly enough with the brutal schedule Gunnar had insisted. They switched drivers every three hours to keep fresh eyes on the road. One of the others would rest in the back while the other stayed awake with the driver. During that time, Linda had had a chance to talk with Jake and be grilled by Gunnar alternately. She much preferred the former over the latter, though both were disconcerting. She found that, as the hours flew by, she liked Jake more and more. Not just as a larger-than-life, sexy male, but as a genuinely likable person.

Then he'd start flirting with her when Gunnar was asleep. Nothing too overt -- what could they do in a moving car with his brother in the back seat? While it irritated Linda, it also titillated her. A taste of the forbidden, so to speak.

When they finally stopped for more than a quick bathroom break and to gas the car, Linda was mentally and physically exhausted. The little town was about twenty-five miles or so from Nogales. Patagonia boasted less than one thousand residents and not much else. Still, it was a quaint little town. Quiet enough to rest before they met up with the other two team members later that evening.

"Noah will meet us in exactly four hours," Gunnar said as they headed to the motel rooms Jake had procured for the night. "I suggest sleep." He raised an eyebrow at Jake. "Make sure your head's in the game." When he glanced at Linda, she wanted to crawl under the SUV they'd driven. Or bitch-slap Jake. "Hers too." When Jake glanced at Linda, she gave him a scathing look. He only grinned at her. Which nearly made her combust. The man was simply devastating on her senses. Worse, he knew it.

Gunnar stomped off. The man seemed never to smile and to always be angry about something. Jake, on the other hand, never seemed to be in a bad mood. Nothing fazed him yet he was still hyper focused on whatever he set his mind to. Right now, all that focus was on her.

He took her hand, gripping it tightly as he walked her inside the motel. When he opened the door to let her in, she thought she could make a quick escape from him by simply closing the door with a crisp "Good day." Unfortunately, he shouldered his way past her, dumping their bags beside the dresser as she just stood there gaping at him.

"What the hell are you doing? You're not staying here."

"We're only going to be here a few hours. The only reason we got a second room is to give you privacy from Gunnar."

"You could stay with him."

Jake nodded. "Yeah. I could. But he snores."

Seeming to dismiss the whole conversation, Jake retrieved a clean shirt and gym shorts from his bag. After disappearing in the bathroom for a couple of minutes, he came out, dirty clothes in hand. "Bathroom's all yours."

With a sigh, Linda decided to use the time alone to recoup and reset. The fact was she was exhausted. Sparring with Jake now would only tire her further and frustrate her to boot. She needed sleep. And a hot shower.

She piled her long hair on top of her head to keep it dry. Sleeping with wet hair wasn't even an option. The hot water sluicing over her skin was heaven. The drive had been harder than she'd been willing to admit. It didn't escape her notice that Jake had hurried to change his clothes to leave her the bathroom. Had he known how sore and knotted her muscles were or had he merely wanted to lie down? Knowing Jake, the infuriating man, he'd known she ached all over. He was observant like that. His focus on her made her feel like she was the only person in the world. How was she supposed to be around him and not fall completely under his spell?

Exhausted, exasperated, more than a little frustrated, she dressed in soft cotton shorts over her boy-short underwear and a T-shirt over her sports bra. She longed to strip off everything and lie naked under the sheets, but it was a motel. And there was a man in the room she was trying to resist instead of entice.

She exited the bathroom only to find Jake stretched out on one side of the king sized bed, legs crossed at the ankles, arms behind his head. As if he were just waiting for her to leave the bathroom and start a striptease or some shit. He gazed at her with half-closed eyes, and the sultry expression in those blue-green depths nearly put her to her knees. Could the man be any more insufferably sexy?

"I'm not sleeping in that bed with you." Best to get that out of the way if she were going to stand her ground. It was as much for her benefit as his because she *did* want to strip for him and wrap herself around him in that big bed and see what happened next.

"Relax, honey. I'm not going to ravish you in your sleep, much as that prospect appeals to me." His lips curled into that stupid grin that did funny things to her insides. "We both need sleep before we meet up with Noah and Tyson. This bed is big enough to put three people between us. There is no reason you wouldn't be perfectly safe on the other side of the bed underneath the covers. I'll sleep on top of them waaaaaay over here." The fucker *winked* at her!

Exhausted as she was, there was no way she was going to win this argument. She just didn't have the fight in her. "Fine. But I'm warning you now. I need you to help find my sister. If you so much as turn over too far on my side of the bed and accidentally brush my hair, I won't kill you, but I *will* castrate you. You don't need your balls to find my sister."

"I always knew you were a dangerous woman. Do you have any idea how sexy that is?" She couldn't help but glance at Jake's crotch. Sure enough, he had a rather large hard-on. Naturally, he found it amusing as hell that she'd taken the bate. "Made you look."

"Ooh, I should gut you!" She picked up a pillow he'd tossed to the end of the bed and hurled it at his face. He caught it and dropped it to the floor, chuckling all the time.

Like it or not, she was getting in on the opposite side of the bed. Once under the covers, she fell instantly into a sound sleep.

***

Jake woke to the unmistakable scent of Linda surrounding him. An unfamiliar weight on his midsection puzzled him. Opening his eyes, he found her curled on her side against him, her dark head resting on his abdomen, one arm thrown over his chest, the other circling his waist where she rested her hand on his ribcage. She was sound asleep.

There was no way to quell the instant erection. How long had he imagined her like this? OK, so not in this particular position, but this was better than his imaginings. She hugged him close like she might a lover. Jake desperately wanted to be that lover. Not for the sex, though he was sure that would be life altering. Because he wanted this woman with all his heart. She was *the one*. He knew it with every fiber of his being. The need he had to claim her, protect her... pleasure her... was nearly overwhelming.

And here she was. Wrapped around him like a blanket. Her silky hair fanned out over them both where it had come loose from the knot she'd fastened it into on top of her head before coming to bed. Now, all that black silk seemed to tie them together.

He had to be careful here. He'd promised her he wouldn't move, but there was no way he could keep from burying his hand in her hair. Other than that he lay perfectly still. Linda obviously needed this for some reason. He would provide. No matter it cost him a painfully hard dick.

He grinned. When she woke -- and she would wake in this position -- he could just imagine the sparks. God, his woman was fierce! What Delta wouldn't be proud of this kind of woman? She was driven, brave, curious, and protective. He could imagine her giving their male children as much trouble as he'd give their girl children.

Funny how he never questioned his tie to Linda. He'd taken on the role of her partner and future mate without hesitation. Maybe it was in his family makeup. Maybe he needed to consult his Uncle Leland. Who would likely refer him to his Aunt Vivian, but he had to try to start out with the male side of the Carvers. They had to stick together, after all.

Just as he relaxed, Linda stirred. That sexy little moan as she woke nearly caused him to thrust his hips in want, but he managed to hold still. Every muscle in his body tensed aggressively.

***

God, something smelled wonderful. Linda inhaled deeply of something that smelled like fresh rain, forest, and warm man. Had there ever been a pillow as perfect as this? It seemed to have the perfect amount of firmness to it, cradling her head but not letting her sink too deeply into it. She hugged it to her as she exhaled contentedly, snuggling closer.

Which was when she felt something pulse under her forearm where it curled over the top of her pillow. Startled, she opened her eyes...

To find herself draped over Jake. Not, like, cuddled into his side where she could have pretended he'd positioned her. Oh no. She was lying possessively over his abdomen, her arms clutching him to her as she might her own man if she had one. That she'd been the one to move in her sleep wasn't in question. Jake lay exactly where he had when she'd climbed into bed. On his side of the big king size bed. She'd sought him out in her sleep. Sure, his hand was buried in her hair, but under the circumstances, she didn't feel like she could say anything.

Linda knew she needed to move. If she were lucky, he was asleep and she could roll off him without making a scene and he never had to know. Except, his cock now pulsed insistently under her forearm. Could this be any more embarrassing? And the *size* of him! Surely she was misjudging what she was feeling. Gingerly, she raised her arm slightly to look. Nope. She hadn't misjudged. He was definitely larger than when she'd seen his lazy erection tenting his shorts earlier. Now, he was completely and totally hard. No question about it.

Before she knew what she was doing, a wicked thought stuck in her head and implanted like a parasite. She could satisfy her curiosity. All she had to do was ease the waistband of his pants over that mouthwatering erection and she could gaze to her heart's content. Even if he was awake -- as she suspected -- he wouldn't stop her. She knew without a doubt he wouldn't stop her.

As if in a trance, Linda watched as her hand slid down his hip to curl her fingers in the elastic. The backs of her trembling fingers brushed the flesh near his cock. Slowly, she tugged. A groan escaped Jake just as Linda whimpered.

Before she could reveal what she was sure would be the most beautiful cock she'd ever seen, Jake's hand covered hers, stopping her even as he gave a deep, rumbling growl. When she tried to pull away, Jack held her hand fast.

"Don't pull away from me."

"I'm sorry," she said, her voice shaking. "I shouldn't have done that. "

"In a different situation I'd not only have let you, I'd have encouraged you." Jake stroked her hand with his thumb, his fingers alternately opening and closing in her hair.

"We should get up," she said, rolling over. He let her until she was off him, then his arm snaked around her waist and Jake pulled her back to spoon against her. She squirmed in a halfhearted effort to get away, but he only wrapped both arms around her and settled her snugly against him.

God, his arms felt incredible! Her head was pillowed on one while it curled around her body to her shoulder. Wrapped up so tightly, she felt protected. Safe. Like as long as she lay like that, within Jake's arms, nothing could touch her. The feeling was more welcomed than Linda wanted to admit or could ever have imagined.

"We have an hour before we need to get up to meet Noah and Ty. Let me hold you until then." He made the demand a request, even as his arms tightened around her. Linda snuggled into him with a sigh.

"Why?"

"Because you're mine. I protect what's mine."

"I don't need your protection. I can protect myself."

"I know."

Linda had no idea why his words warmed her inside or why she truly wanted to be his. All she knew was, this could never happen again. Shouldn't be happening now. But, God, it felt good!

Vowing this would be the last time, she closed her eyes to enjoy the next hour before they planned the move to find her sister.

CHAPTER FOUR

"It's not going to be easy," Tyson said, gesturing with his knife in between cuts at his steak. "She's being kept just outside of town. It's not heavily armored, but the guard is insane."

"The element of surprise should get us in, but getting out will be a bitch if there is any kind of alarm sounded." Noah watched with a raised eyebrow as Tyson gulped down his food, his attention seeming to be focused on the other man completely. "She's a prisoner, but not treated unkindly. It seems Cortez was unable to come to a decision as to how to treat her."

"I'd have thought he'd hate her. Esperanza isn't his child, but the child of another man who fucked his woman." Gunnar didn't try to soften his presentation, and Jake would have liked to punch him in the balls, but he knew better. Gunnar was pushing Linda. Wanting to see how far he could go before she pushed back.

"He probably does. Hence the prisoner part," Tyson continued through a mouthful of meat. "But his in-laws are the real muscle behind his cartel. And they love their daughter. Apparently, they consider Esperanza theirs, no matter what Cortez wants. I wouldn't count on that holding, though. Cortez needs to hold his local group together. Having Esperanza around probably isn't good for his rep. Not sure how or why he's kept her around this long, but I'm sure his in-laws have everything to do with that little decision."

"This could get tricky," Gunnar said, shoveling food into his own mouth. "What's the compound like?"

"Damn straight it could get tricky," Tyson continued. "The compound is relatively unprotected from a defensive standpoint. There are concrete walls around it on all but one side, but no reinforcements and only one tower. Their strength is in the form of sheer numbers. They're moderately armed, but have at least a hundred men guarding the place inside and out."

"Only part time," Noah said, his voice deep but soft.

"Beg your pardon?" Gunnar said, his full attention on the other man.

"The guard is only at the compound in that number part time."

"I got that. What I mean is --"

Tyson cut him off. "He means spit it the fuck out! I've listened to his half-talking and 'the Great Spirit tells me' for a solid month. Say what you mean and get the fuck on with it already!"

Jake couldn't help a chuckle. Noah was a little eccentric sometimes, but Jake suspected he exaggerated it when Tyson was around just to irritate the big man. One look at Gunnar's impassive, unamused face and he suppressed his humor.

"They send wire to Kentucky four truckloads at a time," Noah continued. "Each truck has four vehicles of at least two men each protecting it. I've noticed some trucks head out with as many as four men to each car. I suspect those trucks haul more than just drugs."

"Wouldn't that be a bit obvious?" Tyson reasoned. "A truck barreling it down the interstate with four armed vehicles as escorts just screams 'normal' to me."

"They spread out," Noah continued. "The whole convoy might be spread over several miles. That way, they can head off trouble." He focused his gaze squarely on Gunnar before he spoke again. "Some trucks head out with as many as four guards per escort."

"You think those times the trucks are hauling people for sale." Gunner didn't make it a question.

"I can't be sure, but I have a feeling that may be so." Noah's gaze remained steady. "I tipped off local authorities in Texas, but I suspect they either aren't concerned or they are being paid to look the other way."

"I'll report all this back to the old man. This is bigger than the four of us can handle."

"Leave it up to Noah to uncover a vipers' nest," Tyson muttered.

"Our focus is on Linda's sister," Gunnar said. "We'll take care of the rest later." The gleam in his eyes said they would most certainly take care of business later. "How often are their shipments, Noah?"

"They seem to make a run every week. At least, the last month they've left on Monday morning, each departure staggered out several hours and return on Friday. By Tuesday morning, at least half their guard is on the road, and the group as a whole has more muscle than discipline or brains."

"What are the consequences if we break in there and kill a bunch of motherfuckers?" Jake asked.

"If we're caught, we're on our own. No support. No affiliation. Hawthorn can't take responsibility because of his former military ties, and we're invading a foreign country without sanction."

"In other words, we'll be fucked," Jake supplied.

"You expected otherwise?" Tyson asked with a raised eyebrow. "Anything else would be too easy."

"It is easy," Gunnar snapped. "Simple solution with only one instruction, and I expect all of you to follow it."

"Let me guess." Linda sat back, crossing her arms over her chest. "Don't get caught."

Gunnar pinned her with his gaze, pointing his steak knife at her. "Exactly." He nodded once before resuming his meal. "Girl might just fit in with us, Jake."

"Of course she will."

Tyson and Noah glanced at each other. "She will?" Tyson said, obviously also voicing what Noah was thinking, if the look on Noah's face was any indication. Jake outwardly cringed as much as he inwardly puffed his chest out.

"Well, I don't see *that one* letting Jake leave her behind. I've already been abandoned by one brother. I won't have another one leaving." Gunnar shrugged as if it were nothing. This was it. His team knew. Damn Gunnar for forcing his hand, but God love him even so.

There was a beat of silence then Noah and Tyson started throwing good-natured punches around the table at Jake.

"Way to go, bro!"

"Always knew you liked women who could kick your ass."

"I will fuck both of you bastards up six ways to Sunday." Jake's response, or something like it, was expected. Far be it for him to let the guys down.

Tyson grinned. "At least we know we won't have to worry about you fucking up and getting captured. She'd probably do worse to you than the cartel could ever do if you got careless."

***

"Don't read more into this than there is," Linda interrupted the good-natured ribbing. "I'm not even sure I want to be part of this team, and I damned sure don't intend on being in a relationship with Jake. Just get that out of your head." Jake, the bastard, winked at her. Obviously, she wasn't getting her point across. Her mind drifted back to waking up in his arms before they met with the team. It had felt more right than she felt comfortable acknowledging. "Let's get back to the part where the place they're holding my sister has half the men hanging around."

"Told you," Jake said, grinning at Gunnar. The older man scowled as if he'd just been proven wrong and didn't like it.

Linda raised a brow at Noah, who continued. "The first truck should leave in a few hours. The guard is on alert the first few hours, but later into the night, and especially, the next night, they become more complacent. That's when we should strike."

Gunnar looked to Tyson. "Is that your assessment as well?"

Tyson nodded. "I concur. Should be fairly straightforward."

The other men groaned. Even Gunnar dropped his head into his hands as if Tyson's words physically affected him.

"You just had to say it, didn't you?" Jake glared at Tyson, who merely shrugged as he speared a piece of steak.

Tyson grinned. "Sorry."

Linda gritted her teeth. "Is this a game to you?" she bit out. "I realize it's simply superstitious bullshit, but this is my sister's life you're joking about!" The grin on Tyson's face faded, and he looked contrite, but Linda wasn't buying it. She was definitely on edge. Normally, she could take the kidding around even if she didn't think it appropriate or appreciate it. Now, because of the sexual frustration between her and Jake, she was wound so tight she was ready to snap.

Before she could say or do anything more to embarrass herself, she wiped her mouth and stood. They could plan all they wanted. She had the information she needed. With a little luck, she'd have Esperanza out of there and safely back across the border before they got out of bed the next morning.

CHAPTER FIVE

"You know he was just kidding," Jake said as he entered their room a few minutes later.

"I know all about Murphy's Law and how to invoke it. Though I don't believe in the latter, I don't believe in borrowing trouble either." She had readied a pack as soon as she'd returned, knowing Jake would follow her soon. The last thing she needed to do was tip her hand to her plans. If Jake suspected she was thinking about heading out on her own, he'd try to stop her. Then she'd have to hurt him. Then Gunnar would get involved, and the whole situation would go to shit in a hurry.

"There's nothing to worry about," he said reassuringly. "Noah and Tyson are the best at recon I've ever seen. The two of them could plan an assault on Fort Knox and succeed with the right equipment."

"I'm not worried about that," she said. "Gunnar wouldn't have sent them if he didn't trust them, and Dad wouldn't have put Gunnar in charge if he didn't think he knew how to get the job done."

Jake grinned. "See? You're already accepting us."

"Look, Jake. You seem sure about this, but I'm telling you, I'm not. Like, at all."

"Why? You're good at what you do. So are we. We're all a bunch of Alphas who don't like to be pushed around, and so are you. You'll fit in perfectly."

She scowled at him as she stalked across the room. "Sure. With your team. But you're leading them all to believe we're a couple. We're not."

"Think that all you want, baby. It doesn't change what is."

"Dammit, Jake! I can't do this! I can't be your dirty little secret, and I can't be part of this team with you."

"Why? You're one of us. An elite. You belong with our group." Jake looked sincere, she'd give him that. He believed every word he was saying. What he didn't understand, what she couldn't tell him, was that if she let herself become part of his team and let him into her life, when they split, Jake could very well be the kind of man to take her heart with him.

"Because I just can't," she snapped. "I don't sleep with co-workers. It's awkward when it ends, and in this business, awkward equals dead!"

"Haven't you figured out yet I'm in this for the long haul? This thing between us isn't something everyone experiences, and I'm not an idiot. I'm not throwing it away, so no need to worry about anything being awkward at work."

"Bullshit," she spat. "Bull*fucking*shit! I've seen the women hanging all over you when we were in Rafe's club. I know the kind of women who gravitate toward men like you, and I know what kind of man you are, Jake Carver. I'm not your type."

He lunged for her, circling her throat with his hand, and pressed her back against the wall. It was like someone punched her in the gut the lust hit her so hard. This was the male she longed for. Dominant. Willing to take what he wanted.

Baring his teeth, he loomed over her, leaning close to look her in the eyes. "What kind of woman do you think I want, Linda? What is it you think will satisfy a man like me?"

He seemed to be challenging her. Wanting her to lay out all her reasons they could never be together. She knew it was a bad idea. Knew that, once she did, he'd find a way to refute it, and then what would she do? Still she pushed on.

"A submissive! You'd want a submissive to be at your beck and call in bed. Maybe not out of bed, but you'd demand I submit to you, and it's just not in me to do that!" Once started, she couldn't seem to stop herself. "I'm an aggressive lover, Jake. I take what I want. Any man who can't handle that doesn't have a chance at even one fuck with me!"

She expected Jake to balk, even to back away from her. Instead, he leaned in closer. Closer. Until his lips brushed the tender flesh of her neck. Then he bit down. Not painfully, but a warning nonetheless.

"Understand me, Linda. I want you exactly the way you are." He bit down again on her neck before backing off, laving the small sting with his tongue. "I want a lover who isn't afraid to wake me up in the middle of the night if she needs my cock. I want a lover who wakes me up with head only to demand I eat her in return. My woman will always demand from me what she wants because she'll want the same from me. And, most of all, I want my woman never to be afraid to tell me what she needs because it's the only way I could ever be sure I was satisfying her every want and desire." He framed her face in her hands as he looked into her eyes, holding her gaze. "*That's* the kind of woman a man like me needs, Linda. Are you that woman? Are you that aggressive of a lover? Because if not, you better stop me now. That's what I'll demand of you."

Almost before he finished speaking, Linda lunged for him, fusing her mouth to his. Wrapping her legs around his waist, she held him to her as tightly as she could. Fingers threading through his hair, she forced him where she could better kiss him. Deeper. Harder.

His tongue met hers aggressively, not put off in the least by her demands. The lust seemed to build and build between them with every sweep of his tongue against hers. Never had she experienced such depth of feeling, such an emotional connection to another. The kiss seemed magical in its intensity, bonding them with invisible ties she knew she'd never be able to undo.

Jake maneuvered his hands between them to find the edges of her blouse. With one hard yank, he ripped it open, scattering buttons everywhere. His hands found and squeezed her breasts through the lacy bra. His thumbs found her nipples and brushed, a seductive touch in the middle of such intense hunger.

"Does this feel like I want a submissive lover?" Jake's growl sent chills through her. The kind of chills that wet her panties. "I need a hard lover. One who can give as good as she takes."

With a wanton cry, Linda tugged his shirt from his waistband and whipped it over his head. Her fingers found hair-roughened skin over hard-as-steel muscle. She ached to rub her bare breasts over him, to abrade her nipples with all that magnificent male flesh.

Once the idea was in her head it became an obsession. She couldn't get the front clasp undone fast enough or take the time to let the flimsy material fall from her arms once she did. Linda mashed herself against Jake's hard chest with a groan of sheer delight. His snarl and the bite of his fist in her hair only fueled her lust. She had to have this man. Had to fuck him until she was sated.

"That's it," he growled. "Take what you want, you little bitch."

Linda bared her teeth at him before grasping his chin in her hands and kissing him again. She nipped his bottom lip before thrusting her tongue inside his mouth for a thorough taste.

Jake mashed her against the wall, wedging his jeans-covered cock firmly against her cunt. She needed her fucking jeans off, but separating from Jake for even that short period of time wasn't even an option. She needed. *Needed*!

Then he moved against her. One thrust of his hips, and Linda screamed in ecstasy. Tightening her legs around Jake, she used the leverage to rub her cunt over his cock, giving herself the pleasure she craved. His body provided everything she needed and more. His breath was hot against her ear as he growled and grunted. The way his hair brushed her face, his chest hair abraded her nipples -- all of it made her crazy. It was as if she'd been starving for this man her entire life and was only now partaking of what he offered.

"Fuck!" A scream burst from her lungs as her orgasm started. "Fuck!" The pleasure was so intense her vision tunneled and spots appeared around the edges as she came in a hard, fast rush. Her head spun as she pushed through the orgasm, needing it to last as long as she could make it. Jake's arms tightened around her as his own breathing sounded in harsh, ragged gasps in her ear.

"That's it," he bit out. "Keep coming. I'm going to make you do this all fucking night."

"Bastard," she gasped. "What the fuck are you doing to me?"

He didn't hesitate when he answered, "Making you mine."

Before she could deny his claim, another orgasm overtook her, and all Linda could do was scream.

***

When she loosened her hold on him, Jake moved away from the wall to the bed. God, how had he managed to keep from coming in his fucking pants? The woman in his arms was so far beyond anything he'd ever hoped or dreamed of he wasn't sure how he was going to make it through the night without coming his balls off. He hadn't even gotten her naked, and already he was damned near losing his mind.

He'd intended to strip them both and explore her at his leisure. Instead, he covered her body with his, continuing to thrust against her as he kissed and kissed her.

God, would he ever get enough of her mouth? She kissed him back just as greedily as he kissed her, little whimpers and moans escaping with every thrust of her tongue. Jake tangled his fingers in all that glossy, black hair. The silky strands fanned out around her over the pillow, catching on the stubble over his jaw as if to tie them together.

Reluctantly he pulled himself from her lips to trail down her neck. He was rewarded when his lips found one stiff nipple and closed around it. Linda arched into his touch, just as he'd hoped she would. Her nails bit into his shoulders, one hand fisting in his hair. With a decisive move, she pulled her breast from his mouth only to force his head to the other. Jake happily sucked her nipple, flicking it with his tongue. One hand found her other breast and tweaked the tip, pulling and tugging as he sucked.

"Ah, fuck!" Linda cried her pleasure. "So good!"

"Unh!" Jake's pleasure seemed to be feeding off Linda's. With every cry from her, every arch of her body against his, Jake found it harder and harder to hold himself in check. He desperately needed inside her. Needed to come like he never had before in his life.

Wrapping his arms around Linda, Jake kissed her torso, kissed the fine muscles rippling beneath her skin as he moved down her body to her navel. Linda pushed against him, her legs wrapping around him. Jake knew she was trying to get friction on her clit, but he wasn't letting her come again with her pants on. Oh, no. The next time she came it would be with his mouth firmly attached to her pussy.

Pushing away from her was the hardest thing Jake had ever done. He wanted her pleasure above his own, but he had to get them both naked. He needed to explore her body, to know every secret hollow so he could pleasure her that much more.

"What the fuck are you doing?" Linda panted, her legs still firmly locked around him. Jack bared his teeth at her as he unwrapped her legs, his fingers fumbling with the button on her jeans.

"Get your fucking pants off!"

Immediately, she shimmied out of the rest of her clothes, allowing him to do the same. He shoved Linda back onto the bed, pinned her hips with his hands, and buried his face between her legs. The moment he did, Jake knew he'd found heaven.

Linda screamed the second his tongue flicked her clit. There was no restraining his primitive response. It was as if the dams of emotions and sexual aggression they both held inside them had burst, unleashing a torrent of lust and need so strong neither of them could contain it any longer.

Digging her heels into the bed, Linda rolled her hips off the mattress. Jake tried to hold her down, but she refused to be denied what she wanted. Jake couldn't help but grin. He'd demanded she give him everything she had. She'd delivered. This was Linda. Raw. Primal. *His*.

When her pussy spasmed, her clit pulsing under his tongue, Jake thrust two fingers inside her, curling them to rub deep inside her until she thrashed and gasped on the bed. It took everything Jake could do to stay with her, to help her ride out her orgasm. She bucked hard, moving against his mouth with sinful whips of her hips.

The second the spasms lessened around his fingers, Jake crawled up her body and covered her with his own. He barely remembered to snag a condom from the bedside where he'd put them earlier and sheath himself before shoving into her with a brutal thrust.

Linda gasped at the intrusion, but quickly wrapped her arms and legs around him tightly. Jake wasted no time, surging inside her over and over, driving both of them to the edge once more only to hold them there. Sanity threatened to slip completely from his grasp, but he used an iron will honed in the fires of battle to keep them teetering on the very brink.

"Jake!" She trembled in his arms, sweat beading her forehead and upper lip. Tasting her lips again, while he was inside her, was the only thing he could think of. His tongue thrust as deep, catching her cries as he fucked her. He continued to keep them both on the razor's edge, sanity just as out of reach as relief.

"You need to come?"

"Uh huh!" Her confession wasn't much more than a moan.

"Look at me," he snapped. Her eyes opened slowly, their focus questionable, but she was trying. "You belong with me."

"Jake --"

"And I belong with you. You can deny your feelings or mine, but don't even try to deny what's between us." He gave another shove inside her, making them both groan. "You think you can feel like this with any other man?" At the thought, Jake bared his teeth in aggression.

"That's none of your business."

"It is!" Jake began a hard, steady ride designed to push them both over the edge. It was now or never. He'd take her to bliss and dare her to deny what she felt. Punctuating each word, he bit out, "We. Are. One!"

"NO!" Linda thrashed beneath him, but her hips continued to meet his thrust for thrust. Her nails scored his back and shoulders until she finally moved them to his ass. With a defeated sob, she gripped him hard, her nails digging in like spurs to a horse. She pulled him to her with each brutal surge of his hips. Harder and harder until finally...

Bliss!

Linda's cunt spasmed around Jake, milking him hard for the seed he'd kill to give her. Her scream barely registered over the roaring in his ears as he fought off his own imminent orgasm. Jake was sure he'd lose his mind out the tip of his dick. The orgasm rolling through him promised to be nothing short of cataclysmic. Once her contractions began to subside, Jake let go his control, the pleasure he'd edged for so long now undeniable.

When he came, it was explosive. Never had he come so hard or so long in his life. Pleasure pulsed up his spine and back to his balls as he emptied into the condom until it overflowed. A mixture of her fluids and his own bathed his balls when he finally collapsed over her. They were both breathing hard, ragged. Linda clung to him with her arms and legs like she'd never let him go, which pleased Jake immensely.

He kissed her temple, her eyes, the sweat from her upper lip. "Are you OK?"

"I -- I think so," she said, her voice a whimper.

Someone pounded at the door. Loudly.

"Open the fuck up in there!"

"Fuck," Jake muttered.

"Is that..."

"Yeah. Gunnar," Jake confirmed as he kissed her once before rolling off her and dragging on his jeans. A few quick strides to the bathroom, and he discarded the condom as he buttoned his jeans before glancing over his shoulder to see that Linda had retreated to the bathroom before opening the door.

"What the fuck do you want?" If this gave Linda time to think about what they'd done and regret her actions, Jake would fucking strangle his older brother.

"I want you two to tone it the fuck down," Gunnar growled. "You'll get us kicked out, and then what will you do? I'll tell you what you damned sure *won't* be doing. You won't be getting busy with her because we'll all be together, and I refuse to --"

"Shut the fuck up!"

"You do the fucking same!"

As Jake slammed the door in Gunnar's face, he exhaled a shaky breath and thumped his head against the door a couple of times. Brothers. Gotta love 'em.

CHAPTER SIX

Linda stared at her reflection in the mirror. She should regret what she'd done simply because she'd swore to herself she wouldn't get involved with Jake Carver, but she couldn't find it in herself. The sex had been life altering. She had no idea how she'd go the rest of her life without it, but knew she had to. For now, though, maybe she could use this to her advantage. If Jake thought she was at least giving the matter some thought, he might let his guard down long enough for her to leave and go after Esperanza herself.

Before she could gather her wits about herself, there was a light knock at the door seconds before it opened. Jake stepped into the bathroom with her, his gaze firmly on hers as if gauging her reaction.

Fuck, she wasn't ready for this. How could she be? She'd just had the most fantastic sex of her life, and the man who'd shared it with her was looking at her like he'd love another go-around.

He leaned against the doorframe, crossing his arms over his chest. "What are you thinking?"

Linda ducked her head, not ready for him to see her expression. He'd know how much he affected her. If he didn't already. But he might also see straight through her and know she planned on skipping out to save her sister without him or the team.

With a sigh, she turned away from him. "Just give me a minute."

"For what?" His hand settled gently on her shoulder. She hadn't even heard him move. "For you to pull away from me? Please don't, Linda. Give us a chance."

Slowly, he urged her around to face him. Linda took a deep breath, trying to get herself under control enough to go along with him. She just needed to hold herself together for a little while longer.

"You can trust me," he said. "I'm not going to break your heart."

With a raised eyebrow, Linda replied, "Maybe I'll break yours."

Jake grinned. "I'm willing to risk it."

Linda went into his arms willingly. If she only had this night, she'd take it until it was time to leave. Then his lips found hers, and she gave herself up to the pleasure he so effortlessly created within her.

Where the first time had been frenzied and desperate, this time the pace Jake set was slow and gentle, but no less passionate. Before, Linda had felt the need to battle Jake for dominance. Now, all she wanted was to let him drive. She willingly followed his slow, measured kisses and caresses.

Hands on her hips, Jake held her against him, his cock beginning to pulse against her belly with each lazy thrust of his tongue. Before she realized what she was doing, her arms slid around his neck. Her fingers tangled his hair as she kissed him back, reveling in the textures of his lips, tongue, and skin. Had she ever been so inundated with sensation? Had sex ever been this all consuming?

Unable to focus on anything other than the feel of Jake's magnificent body wrapped around hers, Linda surrendered. Completely. Strong arms lifted her, carrying her back to the bed. She sighed in contentment to feel his weight coming down on her. When she left him, this might be all she had to sustain her.

Because she knew in her heart Jake would never trust her again. So she'd cling to the memories they were making, knowing she'd never find another man who completed her the way Jake did.

Urging her legs around his hips, Jake lifted her. The next thing she knew, Linda was on the bed with Jake following her down, his big body pressing her into the mattress. He urged her leg over his hip, and she dug her heel into his buttock. Strong arms locked around her, Jake kissed her neck gently as he rocked against her. His hard body seemed to imprint itself on hers as they moved against each other. The moment was laden with something she couldn't name. Didn't want to name. It would only make leaving that much harder.

His kissed his way to the swell of her breast, lingering there a moment before finding a nipple and swirling his tongue around it. The pleasure was lazy and contented, like they'd done this a thousand times before. She arched to his mouth, soaking up the sensations like a greedy sponge.

When he left her breast, Linda protested, trying to tug him back. Instead, he reached for the nightstand, snagging a condom. Taking the little packet between his teeth, he ripped it open then sheathed himself before covering her fully again.

His gaze seemed to snare Linda's. She couldn't look away from him no matter how hard she tried. "Don't run away from me, baby," he whispered as he took her mouth again. "Don't run. Stay with me."

God, she wanted to! His big, warm body filled her with so much more than just his cock. He seemed be twining himself around her soul as well as her body.

With one easy thrust, Jake slid into her. The sensation was divine. A little slice of heaven. His movements were languid. He was making love to her.

All at once the emotion welling up inside her was nearly overwhelming. Tears burned her eyes and stung her throat.

"What are you doing to me?" Her whispered question was almost a plea. For what? To stop? To never stop?

"Loving you," was his answer in that husky, murmured voice.

"Ah, Jake!" She clung to him while he moved within her, holding him close. If there were a way to hold this one moment in time suspended forever, Linda would have seized it with both hands.

"That's it, baby. Let go. Just let me have you."

If only he meant for right now. Linda had the distinct impression he meant forever. Which wasn't possible. She couldn't let it be.

She chose to pretend he meant for now and gave herself up to the sensations he created so effortlessly within her. Burying her face in his neck, she let out a soft cry, letting her orgasm wash over her in wave after wave of searing pleasure. Jake's cock throbbed inside her with his own release, his ragged gasp further evidence he'd reached his own peak.

Sweating, panting, they clung to each other. Jake didn't roll off her this time, instead continuing to thrust softly for several moments. Linda reveled in his weight atop her, loving how she felt so small next to him. Hopefully, he'd sleep for a while. It would give her time to sneak out if she were careful. One thing she hadn't counted on, however, was how hard it was going to be leaving Jake Carver.

***

The second she started to disentangle her body from his, Jake was awake. He didn't move and tried to keep his breathing as even as possible so he didn't startle her. He debated on calling her out but knew she was the type of woman to do what she wanted. It was the exact thing he'd told her he wanted in a partner, so how could he fault her now?

Truth was, he didn't fault her. She was doing what she felt like she had to. He'd bet his last dollar she intended to go after her sister. Not because she didn't think his team was capable of getting her out, but because Linda didn't want to risk her heart. She wanted away from him but wouldn't leave her sister to the mercy of others, no matter how capable they might be. To be honest, he admired her all the more for it. Didn't mean he was going to let her do it by herself. The team had her back no matter what she wanted.

He watched as Linda quickly dressed. Her movements were efficient and silent, and he was struck again at her beauty. The woman was as graceful as a dancer. Her light brown skin seemed to shimmer in the dim moonlight that filtered through a crack in the drapes. She wound her long, dark hair tightly on top of her head just before she looked back at him. With a sigh, she opened the door and left.

Jake waited only a few seconds before getting out of bed and quickly dressing. It was time to get Gunnar and follow her. At a distance. Very quietly. So as not to get his balls handed to him. He grinned at the thought. The night should prove to be very interesting indeed.

CHAPTER SEVEN

Linda lay on her belly in the brush watching the last truck leave the compound. Sure enough, each truck she'd observed had at least two escorts. She'd identified forty-two guards within the compound. Of those only about ten or fifteen were carrying anything other than a sidearm. If she were careful, she could enter through a small breach in the fence on the west side. From there, there was only one building other than the main house. Finding her sister would be a challenge, but she had several hours. As long as she didn't get caught. Once she located Esperanza, the two could exfiltrate the same way she got in. If all went according to plan, they would be above the compound on the opposite side from where she now lay. The little jeep she had hidden in a natural rock arch ready to get them safely back across the border into the U.S. ready to move.

Using field glasses, she continued to scout the place searching for any sign of her sister. Sweat dripped from the ends of her bangs into her eyes but she blinked it away, not moving so she didn't give away her position.

The night was calm and moonless. The lights from the compound illuminated both interior and exterior, presumably so they could see anyone coming at them from the outside. They obviously weren't expecting any threat to breach their security or they'd have the interior lights off at night.

Another slow sweep over the camp yielded not a sign of Esperanza. Linda began to doubt herself. Had she been a little too rash in leaving Jake and his team behind? She had all the information they had. Didn't she? She was skilled and determined. She would get her sister out of this place no matter what it took.

"Here."

Linda nearly jumped out of her skin. Jake crawled beside her and handed her a throat mic and an earpiece.

"What the fuck?" she bit out in a whisper.

"Well, you can't very well go charging in there with the rest of us if you're cut off from communication," he explained as if this were all part of the fucking plan to begin with. Regardless of the situation, she still took what he offered.

"What are you doing? Did you follow me?"

He crawled up beside her and grinned. "Of course. If you wanted to take point, all you had to do was say so."

"Speak for yourself," came Gunnar's voice through her earpiece. "I lead this team. You get it through your thick skull, Linda, or next time you stay home."

Linda ground her teeth. This wasn't happening. "I've got this," she bit out.

"And now you've got help. Should be that much easier," Jake reasoned. "What have you found out? Have you found a way in?"

Despite her exasperation, Linda was surprised to realize she was more than a little relieved to know the guys had her back. Which only pissed her off even more. But what could she do? She did need their help, no matter what she'd originally thought.

With a loud sigh, she said, "There's an opening in the barbed wire on the west side. It's guarded, but not heavily and not with anyone who knows what they're doing. Dudes mostly smoke and play cards."

"Stand by," Gunnar clipped through her earpiece.

Linda wanted -- needed -- to turn her head to look at Jake but steadfastly refused. Instead she put the field glasses to her eyes and concentrated on the compound in silence.

"You're not getting rid of me that easily, Linda." Jake voice was calm, unperturbed. Like he was simply stating the facts as he saw them. "I'm on you like a shadow." Then he added, "Or a lover. However you want to look at it."

"I'm not doing this with you, Jake," she said, trying to sound as calm as she could. "We had a night. It was fun. It's over. When I get my sister back, I'm headed back to vice. The end."

"We'll see," was all he said. He'd moved up beside her, studying the place through the scope of his rifle.

"There's nothing to see," she snapped. "I don't sleep with co-workers."

"So, we're staying together but you're going back to vice?"

The fucking man even sounded amused. He was dicking with her, but she couldn't help but play into his hands, her temper getting the better of her.

"We're *not* 'together,' at all! We fucked! How is that together?"

"Because we fucked *fantastically*. Great sex equals together. Admit it. You want me again."

"I'm not doing this with you, Jake." She gripped her field glasses harder, trying to concentrate on the compound, looking for another less obvious way in like she knew Gunnar was doing.

The nerve of the man! Just because he was right didn't mean she would admit he was right. The sex *had* been fantastic. It was like everything inside her had been waiting for this man. She *wanted* to be part of his team.

They were all elite soldiers, and there was so much they could teach her. More than that, she wanted to be part of their improvised family. As far as she could tell, everyone treated everyone else like brothers. Rafe's woman was treated like a sister. These men would die for each other. It was there in everything they did. She knew her father thought a lot of each of them, but she also knew that, though they all respected him, he wasn't included in their family unit. She couldn't bear it if they excluded her as well. Pitiful as it sounded, she was more than a little insecure in that regard. Probably because her father had never been the

nurturing type. He was military. The hard-ass.
Her mother had always been the one to show
tender feelings. After she'd passed, Linda had
felt like that part of her life was missing. As
rough-and-tumble as the guys in Jake's team
were, there was always an abundance of
affection. Not conventionally shown, but there
was no doubt they loved each other like a
family.

"You could do it with me if you want,"
came Tyson's voice over the radio. Which was
when she realized their entire conversation had
been broadcast to all the guys.

"I totally hate you right now, Jake," she
muttered.

"As long as you don't hate me," Tyson
said. "We have a date for after this thing?"

"No," Jake answered before she could.

Just to be contrary she said, "Sure, Ty.
Assuming you make it out of here with your
balls intact, we're on."

"Watch that one, Jake," Ty quipped.
"She's vicious."

"Oh yeah," Jake said. "She has fangs and
claws and knows how to use both."

"That's it," she muttered. "I'm killing you
the second we get out of here with my sister
safely with us."

"See?" Tyson said. "Maybe you should leave this one to me, Jake. I'm not sure you can handle a woman like her."

"Trust me," Linda quipped. "He can handle me better than you, Ty. You're fluff underneath. At least Jake pretends to be a hard-ass."

"If the three of you don't shut the fuck up she won't have to kill you, Tyson," Gunnar said. "I'll kill all of you."

Just like that, Linda was at ease. The exchange was just like something a family would do, ribbing their own to ease the tension. She started to shiver, which had nothing to do with the brisk, spring night air. This was the real thing. All of it. Jake. His brothers. His team. *Family*. Before she even realized the thought was there, she recognized she had to have this. She wanted Jake. She wanted his brothers. She wanted to be part of the team. She wanted to be part of the family.

"Linda, follow the wall around the east side. At the southeast corner, Noah says there is a breach in the wall that is unguarded. It's small, but you should be able to fit through it. Once you're inside, Jake can climb over the wall while you hold his cover. Noah and I will follow once you're in."

"Your sister is on the second floor of the building a hundred yards from the wall," Noah informed.

"Once we're inside, Tyson and Noah will cover the outside. I'll follow the two of you in and be your inside cover. Jake, stick to Linda like her goddamned shadow. Get her sister. Get the fuck out. Questions?"

"Yeah," Tyson piped up. "How many of these fuckers are we allowed to kill?"

"None unless fired upon. Otherwise, you don't do anything unless I tell you to. Anyone else?" When no one answered, Gunnar said, "Let's do this."

***

Letting Linda go through the crack in that wall by herself was the hardest thing Jake had ever done. She was totally vulnerable until he made the climb up the wall and was firmly on the ground. The process lasted all of three minutes, but it seemed like an eternity.

Once inside, gaining the second-story balcony of the neighboring building proved relatively easy. Twice men from the compound swept past, but the team got to cover before they were seen.

"Next motherfucker who gets that close, shoot him in the fucking face," Jake whispered.

"That was too close, Ty. Fucker nearly stepped on me."

"You're such a pussy, Jake. He missed you by a good half inch."

"I've got her," Gunnar said. "Take a right in the hallway. Second door on the left. Move!"

Before Jake could even blink, Linda was up and moving through the door into the hall. His heart jumped.

"Slow down!" he hissed. "You're no good to her if you get yourself killed!"

Sidearm in hand, Linda stopped by the room where Gunnar had indicated Esperanza was being held. Her face was a hard mask of determination. Jake realized she'd worn much the same expression when she'd faced him in the bathroom after they'd made love the first time. She was as intent on getting to her sister as she had been on avoiding an emotional connection with him. Which told her much about the depth of her fear of being with him as well as how much she *wanted* to be with him.

Slipping around her to the other side of the door, he caught her gaze. She nodded once, and he tested the knob. It was locked, of course. Jake stepped back before kicking hard with one foot. The door burst open.

Linda was on her way in, but Gunnar shouldered himself around her, taking point yet again. He'd no more than stepped inside than a lamp came crashing down on his head, sending the big man to his knees.

"Fuck!" Gunnar gasped, gun up and arcing wildly as he tried to get his bearings. Jake steadied his arm, lowering his brother's weapon.

A fierce looking woman all of about five-two stood over Gunnar. Glossy black hair flew in all directions as she reared back her foot and let it fly into Gunnar's crotch.

"Bastard!" she bit out. Gunnar snagged her foot as it flew at him again, flipping the girl on her ass. Using her backward momentum, she rolled to feet and was ready to attack once again.

"Esperanza!" Linda yelled. "No!"

The little hellion had spun to deliver a kick to the side of Gunnar's head when Linda's words registered. She altered her move midair to kick the weapon from Gunnar, who lunged for her with a growl and covered her small body with his own enormous one. The girl -- apparently Linda's sister -- got her feet under him and kicked up with all her might, a battle yell erupting from her lips. Gunner went flying over her head, his forward momentum working against him.

"Son of a bitch," he muttered before rolling to his belly to eye the girl wearily. Girl? She was actually older than Linda. Her petite stature made her seem younger.

"Esperanza! He's on our side!" Linda gripped her sister's arm, pulling her away from Gunnar.

Jack tried to cover the door while assessing the continued threat from Linda's sister.

"We're not going to hurt you," Jack said. "But we need to go now."

"All the commotion is likely to bring the guards down on us," Gunnar gasped, obviously still winded from Esperanza's attack. "Noah. Status."

"All's quiet as can be," he replied. "No one seems to have heard your little tiff. Now can we please get the girl and get the fuck out of here? We've been here too long as it is."

"Something not right?" Gunnar said, never taking his focus from Esperanza.

"Not that I can see. I just don't like being this outnumbered in a foreign country. Seems like a recipe for disaster, and this Native American likes actually being on American soil."

"So, that's our cue," Jake said as he urged the women from their corner. "Linda, lead them out the way we came in."

"Are you sure we can trust them, Linda?" Esperanza asked, still eyeing Gunnar.

Instead of answering directly, Linda gave her a side eye and replied, "Would you rather stay here?"

"Point taken."

"If y'all'er done with the debate, can we get the fuck out?" Gunnar drawled with an irritated snarl.

"Careful exiting the building," Tyson informed. "Three armed tangos just rounded the corner."

"Roger," Gunnar said. "Is there a clear way out?"

"Depends on who's in the building," Noah said. "If the room at the end of the hall is empty, you can safely exit from the balcony on the back side. It's not lighted, but I see nothing with night vision."

"That room is for storage," Esperanza informed. "There's an ammo lockup. They were going to put up bars on the windows but Cortez didn't think it was necessary." She sneered as if inwardly getting the last word on some kind of argument.

"That's our exit, then," Gunnar decided.

"Anyone in that room isn't a friendly," Esperanza said. "They'll kill us once they identify us as intruders."

Gunnar glanced back at her. "You seem to know a lot about the place."

"Up until a few weeks ago I was part of the inner circle. Then my grandmother died. We don't think *Lito* will last much longer. Cortez is only waiting for my grandfather to pass as well then he'll kill me. It's why he had me locked up with everyone else. He wanted no mistake with the guard that I'm a prisoner now."

Jack took a better grip on his gun, glancing at Linda. He could see the sympathy in her eyes for her sister. It was obvious Esperanza thought much of her grandparents, and Linda hurt for her. "Let's do this and get out," he said, making eye contact with Linda, needing her to look to him to see them out safely. He wasn't disappointed. Linda bravely held her ground, but Jake could tell she knew this situation was different than any she'd ever been in before.

With another fierce kick from Gunnar, the door burst inward. Jake charged in, swinging the butt of his rifle against the face of the first guard. Linda followed, driving the heel of her hand into the chin of the second guard. He stumbled backward straight into Jake who wrapped his arms around the smaller guy's neck in a chokehold. A few seconds later, the guy was unconscious, sliding to the floor to lie by his companion.

Gunnar opened the door to the balcony. "Do you have eyes on me, Noah?"

"Yeah. Still all clear. There's a couple of guards making a sweep around the perimeter, but it will be a good three or four minutes before they're anywhere near you."

"Can we make it back to the exit point?"

"Stick close to the building. Stay in the shadows, and you should be fine."

"Exfil. Now." Gunnar gave the command without hesitation. Jake lead the way, resisting the urge to snag Linda's hand on the way. She had to know she was trusted to follow orders and he needed to know she actually *would* follow orders.

The climb down was easier than Jake expected. He basically slid down the balcony support to land softly on the ground. Linda wasn't long behind, followed by Esperanza. Gunnar was last on the ground before they all set off around the building.

They were about to reach the wall when a shot rang out. Gunner grunted and stumbled before dropping to his knees and readying his gun.

"Run!" he yelled. Then all hell broke loose.

CHAPTER EIGHT

Linda's first instinct was to cover her sister. She was the only member of the team not armed, but Esperanza had dropped behind Gunnar and snagged the man's sidearm. While Gunnar laid down cover fire, Esperanza covered the big man as they moved steadily backward toward the exit.

"Go!" Jake shoved her toward the wall. While she shimmied through, Jake scaled it with a rope Tyson and Noah had rigged. She looked over her shoulder to see Gunnar and her sister making slow progress backward as they continued to fire. Esperanza dropped an empty clip only to snag another one from Gunnar's pack, reload, and continue to fire.

"Get your sister through!" Tyson yelled. "Jake and I've got Gunnar covered!"

Linda lunged for her sister and dragged her through the opening in the wall while Gunnar slung his gun over his shoulder to make the climb up and over. When he dropped to the ground, he seemed to crumple under his own weight.

"He's hit!" Esperanza yelled.

"Upper arm," Gunnar bit out. "Nothing vital. Run! Over the ridge!"

Spotlights seemed to fill the night. Fortunately, Noah had chosen their entry point with care and cunning. This section of wall wasn't well lit, and the floodlights in either direction didn't adequately cover it. By keeping to the scraggly bushes and grasses over the land, they were able to avoid detection. The gunfire following them was shot blindly.

"We've got to hurry," Tyson said as he slung his pack into the jeep they'd hidden for their getaway. "Gunnar is bleeding all over the place. If they've got dogs, they'll be on us fast."

"So, get us the fuck out of here," Gunnar grated as he crawled in the back, readying his gun even though blood steadily dripped from his arm.

"I'm just over the rise," Noah's voice came over the radio. "Don't leave me."

"Move your ass, Noah!"

"Covering our tracks," he said. "Next time, don't bleed all over the fucking place."

"Tangos coming from the East! We gotta move!" Tyson shouted, gunning the engine.

"Fifteen seconds," Noah panted. Linda readied her gun, squinting to see what Tyson had already spotted. She moved to the passenger's side in the back seat, readying to fire the second Tyson gave the word.

"You don't have that long!" Tyson opened fire through the passenger side open window. There were several shadowy figures running toward them from that direction so Linda took aim, firing steadily. Jake was behind her, firing from above her on the right. Smoke filled the vehicle, making her eyes water, the smell of sulfur as heavy as the smoke. Each *pop* of a discharging gun rang loudly in her ears, but she gritted her teeth and ignored it.

A few seconds later Noah yelled, "Go! Go! Go!"

With a roar of the engine, the vehicle sped off, throwing Linda into Jake. He steadied her with one hand while still firing.

"Fuck!" Gunnar swore as Esperanza tied a strip of her shirt around his arm tightly. "I'm

not bleeding to death. You don't have to -- ah!"
He yelled as she gave a vicious tug, tightening
the strip of fabric over the wound.

"Really? You should look at the mess
you're making! There's blood everywhere!"
Esperanza wasn't gentle in tending Gunnar's
would. She worked in efficient but quick
movements, seeming not to concern herself
with finesse. "Hold still," she snapped, slapping
the back of Gunnar's head when he attempted
to shake her off.

Though her sister had been raised in the
States for the most part, her time in Mexico
must have made it necessary to pick up an
accent. It wasn't much, just a softening to the
edge of her words, but it was definitely there.

As they made their way over the barren
land, Linda noticed they weren't headed back
to the expected crossing. "Where are we
going?"

"If you'd bothered to stay for the whole
briefing," Gunnar bit out, his voice strained,
"you'd know we were headed to a military
crossing. They won't help us, but they won't
stop us either, thanks to the old man."

Just as they topped the rise above the
compound, a massive explosion rocked the
vehicle and lit up the night. Fire rose, billowing
into the sky. Linda nearly dropped her gun in

her haste to cover her ears. Jake pushed her to the floor of the SUV, covering her with his own body.

"What the actual all-fired fuck?" Tyson grated as he shook his head. Though everyone looked toward the compound, wanting to see the destruction, Tyson kept his foot on the gas, never letting up. The explosion was the perfect cover, and the big man wouldn't want to waste it by stopping to observe.

Esperanza checked her weapon, a little smile on her face. She said nothing.

Gunnar glared at her. "What the fuck did you do?"

She shrugged. "I'm not saying I did anything. However, *theoretically*, someone could have rigged the place to blow using a proximity detonator. *If* someone could manage to steal some explosives and the other hardware from somewhere close by without too much notice. Theoretically." When she buffed her nails on her shirt, Linda grinned.

"That's *my* baby sister."

CHAPTER NINE

The ride back to the border was uneventful. Though they barreled down a dirt road in a vehicle running with no lights, the full moon made it easier to see the dirt ribbon that served as a road. Only one jeep pursued them. A couple of shots by Jake had taken out the driver, the truck skidding off the path wildly. It hadn't hit anything, but no one continued with the chase.

"Either that blast in their front yard spooked them or they lost more than they could afford to lose," Tyson muttered. He and Noah continually scanned the barren land for signs they were being followed.

"How much farther?" Linda knew she wouldn't rest easy until they were miles deep into the U.S. She couldn't help worrying for her sister. Would the Cortez family come after the wayward granddaughter? Somehow, she doubted Esperanza would truly be safe no matter how far away from Cortez territory she fled.

"Not far. Just up ahead." Tyson adjusted his grip on the steering wheel while Noah spoke into a radio. The response was a series of mic key-ups but nothing more.

"We're good," Noah said. "Maintain speed, and we'll just drive right through."

The border wall grew larger as they neared it in the moonlight. Sure enough, the gate was open. Guards in two towers on either side of the gate watched on with rifles at the ready, but no one impeded their progress. Seconds later, they crossed the border into Texas. With a relieved sigh, Linda sat back. They'd made it.

While she wanted to put more distance between them and the Cortez family, a sense of relief washed over her. It wasn't until a few minutes passed that she realized Jake had his arm securely around her shoulders.

With a sigh, she laid her head against his shoulder, testing out her new feelings. His arm tightened around her, his chin resting on the top of her head. It felt...right. When Jake kissed her temple something warm unfurled inside her. A little moan slipped out before she could stop it. She tensed, hoping no one heard. When she glanced up at Jake, he was grinned down at her and winked.

***

Was Linda finally giving in to the pull between them? Her fragile acceptance of him warmed Jake's heart. It didn't take long for the movement of their vehicle to lull Linda to sleep. Her breathing even, one hand clutched in his shirt, she rested against him trustingly.

Noah glanced back at them. "How did she plan on storming that place on her own?" His voice was low and soft, obviously not wanting to disturb Linda.

"Not sure she did. I think she knew we'd have her back."

"When this is all done, she and I need to have a conversation," Gunnar grumbled. "She should have been part of the team from the beginning."

"And you know as well as I do that was more my fault than hers. I spooked her," Jake admitted, unwilling for Gunnar to take out his big-brotherly wrath on Linda. Gunnar was their protector. Always had been. When one of his team took themselves out of his reach, it didn't sit well with him. And usually didn't work out too well for the team member in question.

"Then she should have come to me." Gunnar's voice was gruff. He was likely going over scenarios in his head of all the ways tonight could have gone wrong for Linda. For the whole team.

"You know she wouldn't do that. Something like that's too personal to go to someone she barely knows. Besides, you're not exactly the approachable type."

"Why would you expect something like that?" Esperanza's voice held a note of impatience. "That's unrealistic."

Gunnar didn't answer, only turned away from the woman to continue his watch for anyone pursuing them.

"Because he's taken Linda on as one of us. And we're family," Noah said quietly. "Gunnar takes care of his family whether they want it or not."

"Sometimes," Jake continued, "he forgets the rest of us can't read his mind. He also forgets not everyone adjusts to his way of thinking as readily -- and easily -- as he does." Esperanza looked thoughtfully at Gunnar. Jake could almost see the wheels turning in her mind. "Fine," she finally said. "Maybe I'll keep you."

CHAPTER TEN

Dawn was just breaking when Linda woke. She was in a bed, Jake spooning her close. His big, hard body pressed against hers. Strong arms held her securely and pillowed her head. There was a vague memory of being carried, but other than that she had no idea where she was or how long they'd been there. Oh. And she was naked.

Sunlight filtered through the valance covering the window in a soft, muted glow. She could definitely get used to this.

As she lay there simply enjoying the sensations and the feeling of waking up in a man's arms, she reevaluated everything that had happened over the past couple of days.

Jake had seduced her. Successfully. Not only had he won her body, but he'd won her heart, mind, and soul. There was no way she'd ever find another man who called to her on every possible level as Jake did.

She wanted everything he offered. Being part of his elite team, his circle of friends. His family. She'd grown up with her sister, but they'd had to fend for each other. It would be nice to have big brothers to have their backs.

Also, by leaving to get her sister without him, she'd disrespected him and made light of the feelings she'd known he held for her. No way a man could fake that night they'd shared. When he'd found her that night, he hadn't seemed put out, but she knew it had to have bothered him.

"What are you thinking, love?" His rumbly voice next to her ear was pleasing. Arousing.

"I owe you and your team an apology."

She felt him grin at her neck as he leaned down to kiss her shoulder. "Why would you think that?"

"In a different situation someone could have gotten hurt." When he only grunted, she added, "*And* I shouldn't have taken out my fear on them. They were only trying to help, even had everything under control. I could have really messed up because I was running from you."

At her confession he nipped her ear gently. "So, don't ever do it again. Accept I'm in your life to stay, and there'll be nothing for my family to forgive."

"Gunnar was angry."

"Gunnar's always angry about something. Not really, but he always acts angry." Jake chuckled. "He takes his role of big brother very seriously."

"He *is* a bit bossy."

"That he is. But he'll be your staunchest ally. He'll protect you as fiercely as I will. They all will."

"And my sister? I need to see her. If she's back in my life how will the others treat her?"

"Hmm..." He trailed off as if pondering the question.

"What is it?"

"Don't worry about Esperanza much. She's kind of staked a claim on Gunnar."

Linda jerked, flipping over to face Jake. "The hell you say!"

Jake laughed. "I know, right?"

"How's Gunnar taking it?"

"I'm not sure he knows what to do with her. Last I saw them after we stopped here for the day she'd sent him out with specific instructions for her breakfast while she went shopping for a change of clothes. She told him she'd *let* him buy those things for her if he'd promise to bring back the fluffiest pancakes he could find with an obscene amount of whipped cream." Jake's eyes lit up with amusement. Obviously he found the scene he'd witnessed very amusing.

"How'd he take it?" Even though she had other things on her mind just now -- like showing Jake just how hard she was going to try at building a relationship with him -- she found herself curious as to how Gunnar would deal with her sister. Esperanza could be a tad... petulant.

"He swore and got in her face with his finger telling her how he'd be damned if he let anyone give him orders. When she simply raised an eyebrow at him, he grumbled before handing her a credit card and leaving to find pancakes."

"Damn," Linda said, once again feeling her lips tug in a grin.

"Yeah. Gunnar is really a big ole softy. He thinks we don't know, but we do. Your sister couldn't have picked a better man."

"You think that's what she's done? Decided she wants Gunnar?"

"Whether she has or not, I think Gunnar is beginning to think she has. And I'm not sure he's all broken up about it."

There was silence then. Linda reached up to caress Jake's stubble-covered jaw. The man was truly handsome, with the greenest eyes she'd ever seen. "Can I tell you something?" she finally said, knowing she had to get it out before they could move forward.

"Anything, baby." He looked at he like she was the only woman in the world, the love and affection he'd professed earlier all too evident in his penetrating gaze.

"I can't imagine going through life knowing I didn't at least try to have a serious relationship with you. Will you let me give it a good shot this time?"

He grinned down at her, smoothing hair away from her face with a gentle touch. "The way I see it, you didn't have a choice the first time. I pretty much forced myself into your life whether you wanted me or not. Besides, it's not like I was letting this be the end. I'd planned on seducing you continually until you agreed to give me a chance to prove I'd make a good man for you. Also, I figured you'd go after your sister. Not because you really thought we couldn't do the job, but out of loyalty to her. Otherwise, you'd have run so far away from me, it would have been hard to find you. You're loyal and dedicated to your family. We are too, baby."

"Well, OK then." Her grin answered his. "But I warn you, I'm a bitch to live with. I'm moody. And if you leave your dirty underwear in the middle of the bathroom floor, I will suffocate you with it."

"No worries. I was raised in a military home and did my time in the Marines as well. No dirty underwear on the floor. It's a requirement for Delta Force, you know."

"Just so long as we understand each other." Humor faded from her mind as she continued to look into those green, green eyes. "Make love to me, Jake. Please."

"Linda..." His lips found hers on a breath.

Jake's arms tightened around her, those wonderfully delicious muscles wrapping around her, mashing her against more muscle. Had she ever felt so protected? Safe? Jake had come for her when she'd been stupid and running headlong into something she had no hope of handling. Instead of condemning and berating her, he'd simply taken it in stride. Chalked it up to a quirk of her personality, one he admired.

She surrendered to him, letting Jake sweep her into a place where the only thing that existed was the two of them and the pleasure they could give each other. His tongue swept into her mouth to tangle with hers. There was no stifling her moan of need. His answering growl thrilled her. Then she remembered the first time they'd made love.

"Wait," she gasped, pushing him back with one hand while tugging him closer by his hair.

"Don't want to wait," he growled.

"Where are we?" she gasped. "I don't want your brother breaking down the door."

His chuckle sounded strained as he dipped his head to latch on to one exposed nipple. This time, she cried out sharply at the contact.

"Not to worry, my lusty beauty. We made it to southern Tennessee and a family ranch. While the rooms aren't soundproof, the walls are thick, and they put us as far away from everyone as they could. Scream to your heart's content."

With that, he bit down on the nipple he was sucking as he tightened his hold on her roughly. Linda arched her back, her last worry allayed. She'd trust Jake to take care of her. To pleasure her. To make her happy. The instant she made the decision, her heart seemed to expand, filling up with all the love she hadn't even realized had grown in such a short time. She had no idea when it had happened or how she'd been able to deny it, but there it was.

She *loved* Jake Carver!

CHAPTER ELEVEN

The moment Linda surrendered her body and heart, Jake knew it. There was a difference in the way she moved under him. Fine, strong muscles beneath her silky brown skin didn't tremble but bunched with her effort to pull him closer to her.

"My little Spanish Rose." He kissed his way to her other breast, loving the sweet taste of her skin. "My beautiful girl." God, how he loved every inch of her! Not just her body, either. "My warrior woman. You. Are. Perfect."

She whimpered, pulling him back up to kiss him again. "Jake..."

"Everything about you complements me. I love your sass, your loyalty, your passion." He grinned then, raising his head to kiss her nose. "And I love pushing your buttons. When you get angry, there is nothing in this world that is

sexier. Unless you threaten to pull a weapon."
He licked her neck before whispering at her
ear, "Then it's all I can do to keep from ripping
your clothes off, bending you over the nearest
table, and fucking you senseless."

"Well," she whimpered on a breathless
gasp. "When you put it *that* way."

Jake rolled fully on top of her, wedging his
hips between her legs. He thrust against her,
his cock slipping through her lips in a silken
glide.

Forehead to forehead they lay, limbs
entwined, breathing as one. Jake wanted to
draw the moment out, to linger there as long as
possible. Never had he wanted a woman so
badly. Everything about Linda called to him on
an elemental level. Instinctively, he knew she
always would.

Over and over he slid against her.
Through her. The sensations nearly
overwhelmed him. As he rubbed over her clit,
she shivered with each stroke, arching to him
with every thrust of her own hips.

Without warning, she shoved him off her,
pushing him to his back on the bed. He was
about to return the favor when she straddled
his face before engulfing his cock in her hot,
wet mouth.

"Ah! Fuck!" He groaned, the pleasure un-*fucking*-believable.

"Mmmm," she moaned. Blood rushed from his head straight to his groin. Lightheaded, he buried his face between her legs, thrusting his tongue inside her. Linda responded with a long, sensual suck and another, "Mmmm."

If it was possible to lose his goddamned mind through his dick, Jake was certain he was doing it. Linda's mouth on his cock, that thing she was doing with her tongue while she sucked, wasn't something he was prepared for.

"Fucking hell! What are you fucking doing to me?" Had anything ever felt this good?

With a loud pop, she let his cock slip from her mouth. Looking over her shoulder, Linda whispered, "Loving you."

A stunned breath escaped him. Repeating his own words? Could she finally admit she loved him? He couldn't help his grin as he licked her cunt in a long, lingering swipe. "I knew I was wearing you down."

"Shut up," she said between sucks at his cock, "and fuck me."

Who was he to deny her?

With a swat to her ass, he tossed her off him to her back and covered her with his big body. Linda clutched at his sides, scraping her nails over his skin before sinking them into his muscled ass. She raised her hips to meet him as he rocked against her, and Jake broke out into a sweat.

He was about to move off her and put on a condom when the head of his cock met her entrance. For one perfect moment, he was sliding inside her skin to skin but managed to hold himself still before he said fuck it and simply made her his in every way.

"Fuck," he whispered. "Ah, God..."

"Jake," she whimpered. "Do it..."

"Baby, we need to talk about this."

"We are," she said. "I'm telling you to fucking do it." Her voice was a whisper, soft despite how harsh her words were. "Get inside me and fuck me. *Now!*"

"I --"

His words were cut off when she gave him an impatient look, grabbed his ass, and pulled him to her. She met him halfway so his length was completely inside her before he could register what she'd done.

"Fuck!" The word was a stunned, hoarse shout. He dropped his body fully on top of her, moving his hips in a jerky, rhythmic movement. Uncontrollable. Unbelievable pleasure.

Linda writhed underneath him, seeming as desperate as he was. He needed the pleasure her body offered up so freely and sweetly. Craved that closeness he'd only ever found in her arms.

"So fucking hot," he whispered in sweet delight. "So fucking good."

"Jake." She looked at him with wonder, like she was making love with him for the first time. The expression on her face probably mirrored his own. Pleasure like he'd never known overwhelmed him. Not just physical pleasure, but a soul-deep feeling he'd finally found what he'd been searching for his entire life and had never even known he'd been missing.

He found her lips, tenderly licked them. The sweet flavor of her poured into him like the rising tide. The unique honeysuckle scent of her silky-soft skin surrounded him like the comfort of a warm blanket. If he lived to be a hundred, Jake knew he'd always remember this perfect, perfect moment.

When he met her gaze again, she gave him a contented smile as she slid her hands over his back. Her sweet arms circled his neck, and she pulled him back for another kiss.

Jake surrendered his body to her willingly. Eagerly. He might crave her compliance in bed, but he knew he would always bend to her will. It wasn't even a conscious effort on his part. She needed. He provided. Right now, she needed to lose herself in every pleasure he could give her.

As he continued to kiss, Jake worked her body with his, sliding in and out of her at a leisurely pace. Linda rocked against him, her feet bracing on his calves. Jake wrapped an arm around her as he continued to move, bracing his weight on one outstretched arm so it wasn't uncomfortable for her. Nothing could mar this experience for her.

"Oh, God! Jake," she cried out. "It's so good..."

"It's us," he said. "Us together."

"You're so hot. So hard." She arched against him. Wrapping her legs around his waist, she pulled herself against him, fucking herself and using him to do it. "I need you, Jake." She gasped. He felt her pussy spasming around him as she started to come. "So fucking much!" With one final scream, she came, milking him like she intended to take his seed whether he wanted to give it or not.

"That's it, baby. Come so hard for me."

She clung, shuddering over and over as he continued his leisurely thrusting. Each time he withdrew, he felt like her little pussy was trying to pull him back inside. She was so tight. Hot. Wet. The connection they now shared was nearly overwhelming. The need he'd felt since the first day he'd met her amplified exponentially.

Even after she'd come, Linda still clung to him, sliding her legs higher to cross her ankles at the small of his back. With a little sigh, she opened her eyes and smirked at him.

"Your turn, baby." She had her arms around his neck, her fingers tunneled through his hair. Basically, she had him right where he wanted to be.

"Linda," he began, trying to be reasonable when all he wanted to do was plunge himself inside her beckoning heat over and over until his cum was planted so deep inside her there was no way it wouldn't take root. "Is this really a good idea? I don't want you to do anything you'll regret later."

"I never do. Now." She leaned up to whisper at his ear. "Why don't you fuck me until you come deep inside my greedy pussy. Can't you feel it milking you?" For emphasis, she gave a little squeeze of her muscles. "I want it just as much as my pussy does. Don't you want it just as bad?"

"Ah, fuck," he muttered before starting a driving, intense rhythm. There was no way this wasn't happening. She was obviously on the same page he was. Needed the same thing he did. "I'm not asking again," he bit out. "Are you sure?"

In response she squeezed her muscles around him again, arching to meet him. She ground herself on him as he pounded into her. Sweat mingled over their bodies as they were carried away in a mating frenzy. The need to do this, to come in her and stake his claim forever on her, seemed to drown out everything in his brain.

The tingling at the base of his spine warned him he was approaching the point of no return. As he looked at Linda, needing her answer, she met his eyes with her own heavy-lidded gaze. A smile curled her lips as her breath quickened. "I'm going to come, Jake. When I do, it's going to be so hard there will be no way you can hold back from me."

A burst of air left his lungs in a strangled laugh. "As if I could hold anything back from you."

"Then there shouldn't be a problem." Her voice was breathy, her climax a certainty.

Jake kept his gaze on hers, taking in every expression as it crossed her beautiful face. The instant she came, her eyes dilated and her lips parted. A gasp left her throat, followed by a whimper. Finally, her whole body tensed as she threw her head back and screamed.

The spasms around his cock were so intense, Jake bit back a yell. Not long after, his balls tightened. His movements were out of his control, his body taking from hers what it needed to complete his own pleasure. With a brutal yell ripped from his lungs, Jake emptied himself inside her. He shuddered as his cock pumped seed for her. She took it greedily, her cunt gripping him in a stranglehold.

Finally, after what seemed like an endless orgasm, Jake collapsed on top of her. He tried to roll to the side, but she refused to let him.

"No," she said simply. "I like your weight on top of me."

"Don't let me hurt you, baby," he said as he kissed the side of her neck, burying his face there and inhaling her sweet fragrance.

"As if you could." She stretched, wrapping her arms tighter around him. Her lips grazed the side of his face. "Why did I ever think I could stay away from you?"

With a long-suffering sigh, Jake pulled back to look at her. He did his best to keep his lips from quirking in merriment. "It's my sex appeal. I've heard it's just too much for the mere mortal woman."

She didn't even bother restraining her laughter.

ABOUT THE AUTHOR

Erotic romance author by night, emergency room tech/clerk by day, Marteeka Karland works really hard to drive everyone in her life completely and totally nuts. She has been creating stories from her warped imagination since she was in the third grade. Her love of writing blossomed throughout her teenage years until it developed into the totally unorthodox and irreverent style her English teachers tried so hard to rid her of. Now, she breathes life into faeries, space hunters, werewolves, vampires, shapeshifters, and a few just plane ole ordinary people. She loves to see the awkward, self-conscious band geek get the captain of the football team and make him beg for it.

MARTEEKA
KARLAND
Experience the Magic

TWITTER: @MARTEEKAKARLAND

MARTEEKASDESIGNS.BLOGSPOT.COM

FACEBOOK.COM: MARTEEKA.KARLAND

MARTEEKAKARLAND.BLOGSPOT.COM

WWW.MARTEEKAKARLAND.COM

45333600R00073

Made in the USA
Middletown, DE
01 July 2017